How Do
I Love You?

Marion Dane Bauer
Illustrated by Caroline Jayne Church

How do I love you?
Let me count the ways.

I love you as the sun
loves the bright blue days.

I love you as the bee
loves a fragrant flower.

I love you as the thirsty duck
loves a sudden shower.

I love you as the bird
loves a song to sing.

I love you as the waking bear
loves the smell of spring.

I love you as the cat
loves a sunny sill.

And as the dancing snowflakes
love the winter's chill.

How do I love you?
Let me tell you how.

I love you as the nest
loves the sturdy bough.

I love you as the sea

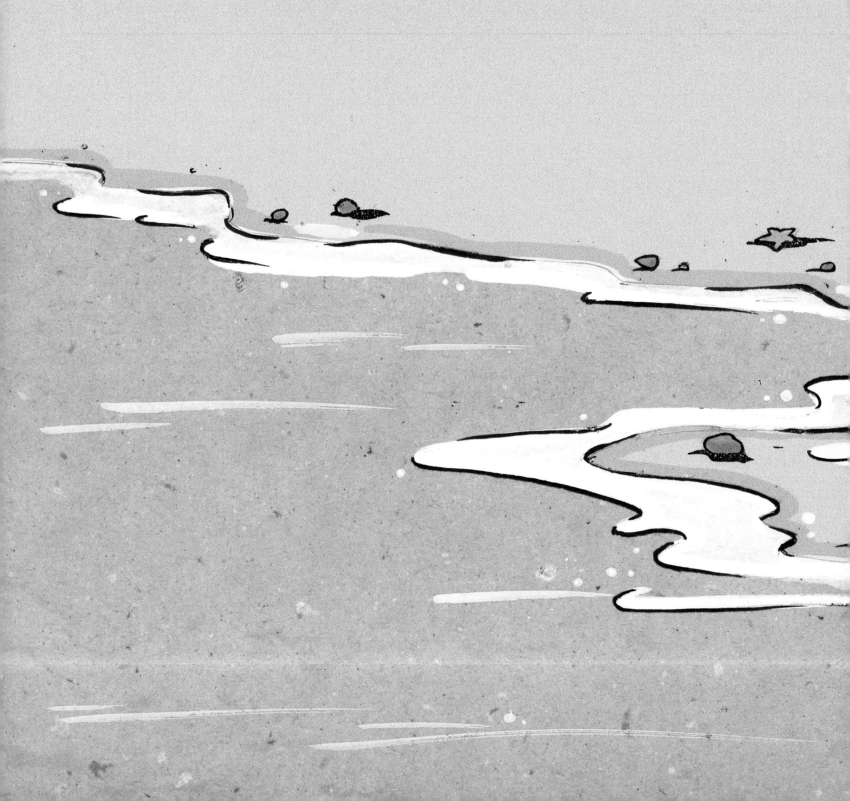

loves the sandy shore.

And as the ancient world
loved the dinosaur.

I love you as the wind
loves its own sweet sound.

And as our friendly Earth
loves to spin around.

I love you as the moon
loves each shining star.

I love all that you will be
and everything you are.

For little
Beatrice
Elizabeth
C.J.C.

First published in 2009 by Scholastic Inc.
This edition published in 2017 by Hodder Children's Books

Text copyright © Marion Dane Bauer 2009
Illustrations copyright © Caroline Jayne Church 2009

Hodder Children's Books
An imprint of Hachette Children's Group
Part of Hodder & Stoughton
Carmelite House
50 Victoria Embankment
London EC4Y 0DZ

A catalogue record of this book is available from the British Library.

ISBN: 978 1 444 92561 6

10 9 8 7 6 5 4 3 2 1

Printed in China

An Hachette UK Company
www.hachette.co.uk